Curious Catwalk

To Aunt Irene

Published by Propeller Press
P.O. Box 729, Fort Collins, Colorado 80522
www.propellerpress.com

Publisher's Cataloging-in-Publication Data
Gravdahl, John.
Curious Catwalk
Story and pictures by John Gravdahl.
1st ed.
p. cm.
LCCN 2001116546
SUMMARY: Nosy the cat takes a quiet morning stroll
which evolves into a full day of adventure and observation
and ultimately makes for an unusual day.
Audience: 4-10
ISBN 0-9678577-8-3

1. Cats--Juvenile Poetry. 2. Children's Poetry,
American. [1. Cats--Poetry.] I. Title.

PS3607.R4284C87 2002 811'.6
QBI33-305

Text of this book set in Freeform 721.
Illustrations created with watercolor pencils and gouache.

Printed in Hong Kong
1 3 5 7 9 10 8 6 4 2

curious
CATWALK

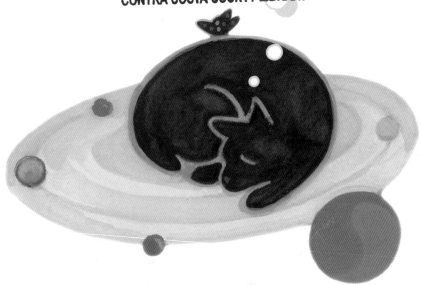

Story and Pictures by John Gravdahl

Oh Cat! What is that?

You wake up from your slumber.

Don't be a lump . . .

Jump!

Watch out and look up, stripes and lights bring a warning. Flat cats are no fun!

Walk with a whisper

like a whisker in the dark,

soft, slow . . .

high and low.

Kitty toes get sore
chasing wiggles up a rope.
Wind and waves below.

Wet paint in the sky,
cats can walk but they can't fly.
Orange pawprints follow.

Tiptoes to the point
and bumpy clouds go breezing.
Tip top heights in sight.

Turn around and find
what's along the other line.
Wings hum in the sun.

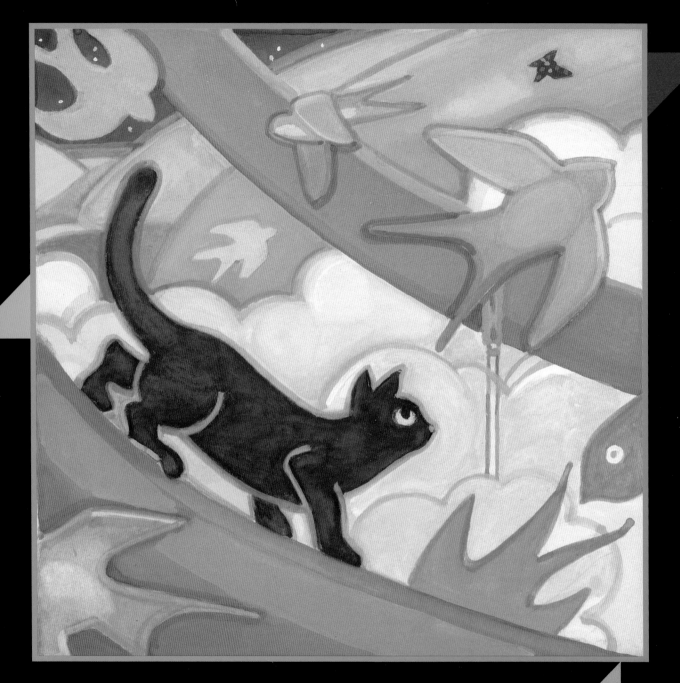

Tummy grumbles now,
flapping feathers flutter too.
Come on feet . . .

Let's Eat !

Purple night sets in
and sudden sights turn silly.
Time to hurry on.

Now, warm lights await.
Stepping down, up and over,
this walk circles . . .

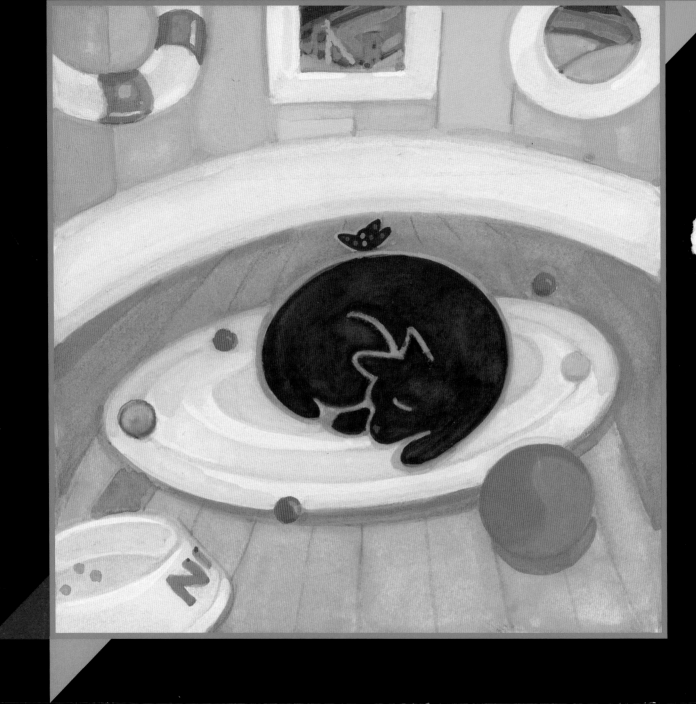

Home.

Good night!